THE
WORRY MONSTER'S
MACHINE

Katie Washbourne

The excitement grew as the time was near,
For the kids to visit the new machine.
It was there to help with worries and fear,
A wonder that really must be seen.

The friendly man said it was blue and pink,
That lights would glow and buttons beep.
There will be a monster to help you think,
To find the answer that you seek.

The worry monster met them at the door,
A furry bundle of joy and fun.
He asked them step onto the floor,
"Come as close as can be done."

"Welcome!" he said, with a growl,
To my machine of wonders and more.
Come and chat, laugh and howl,
At what you have in store.

"What is your name, young one?"
"Elsie," said the little girl, so small.
"Are you ready to have some fun?"
"Yes, but I am afraid I will fall."

One eyebrow rose on the monster's face,
As he heard the word afraid.
"Move to this spot, this very place,
Your worries will be relayed.

I will feed your fear into this slot,
It will travel up and around a bit.
It will spin and spin, wait a jot,
It will be ready soon, just sit!"

Elsie, the little girl scared to fall,
Sat on the floor gripping her feet.
It was hard to fall when sat so small,
Her bottom already on a seat.

She'd fallen once when she was small,
It had hurt her knee so bad.
It was in the past, this fall,
No need to feel this sad.

The monster paused and took a drink
All the children waited and looked
He pretended that he had to think
Making sure they were all hooked.

Drama, just what the monster loved,
He pulled a lever and twisted a dial.
Pushed at a button with a shove,
And up popped an answer in some style.

"Look at the to-do box" he smiled,
"It tells you what you can do,
To overcome the fear you filed,
That stops you from being you."

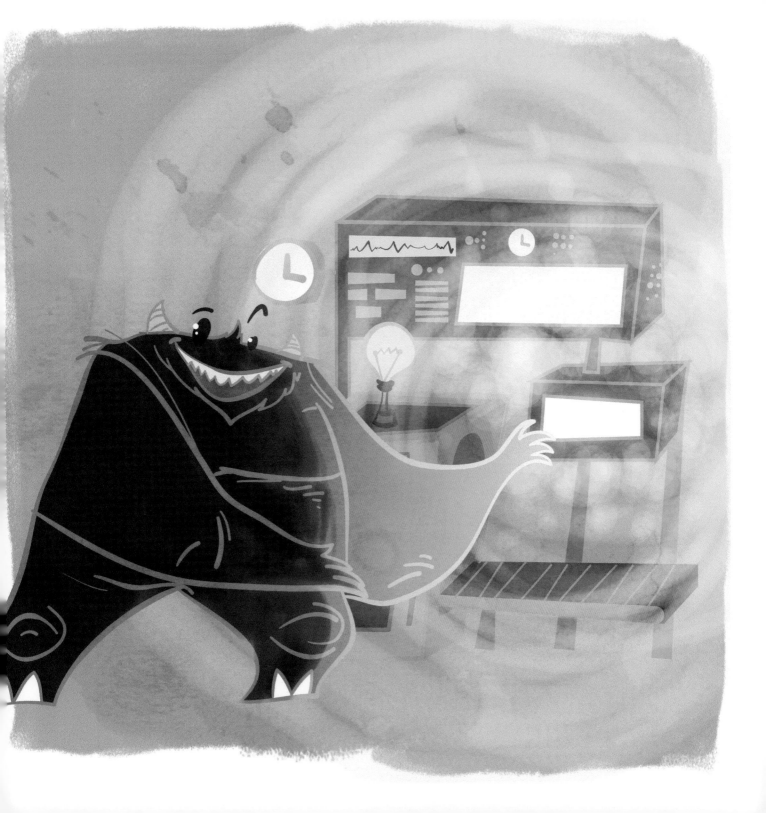

Elsie stepped up and looked at the words,
And read the "to-do" as she was told.
Be confident, it read, like birds,
Who flap their wings so bold!

They do not fear falling from the sky,
As they jump from the nest.
They know that they will fly,
Just like the rest who try their best.

And if one time by chance you fall,
Brush yourself off and stand.
Stretch yourself and feel tall,
You walk more than you land.

Elsie smiled, her worry now gone,
She would walk tall and be sure.
Fall she might, but fear none,
She'd stand again and try once more.

A small voice came from the back,
A little boy so tiny and unsure.
On his back was a bright red pack;
He shuffled forward, wanting more.

"My name is Tom," he declared,
Monster crouched; the voice too low.
Tom shouted, wanting to be heard,
The monster toppled with the blow.

A sudden voice so loud and bold,
Coming from the boy so small.
"Your age, young man, how old?"
"I am 8, just really not so tall."

"I have a worry, I am afraid,
That I will forever be this small.
Tiny is how I have been made,
And I really wanted to be tall!"

Monster's eyebrow rose; a big smile,
He nodded and prodded, with a nudge.
To the slot where the boy should file,
But, the child wouldn't budge.

"I can't reach," he said,
Looking so sad.
His face turning red,
He was upset, a little mad.

"I said I was shorter than could be,
Why did you ask me to reach the slot?
He took off his pack for all to see,
Laying it on the floor, he had a plot.

He stood high on the red pack,
Reaching, he slotted in his fear.
He'd grown taller on the stack,
High enough to glimpse and peer.

As his worry tumbled down the slot,
Spinning round and round.
Up and down and plop,
Until there was this pinging sound.

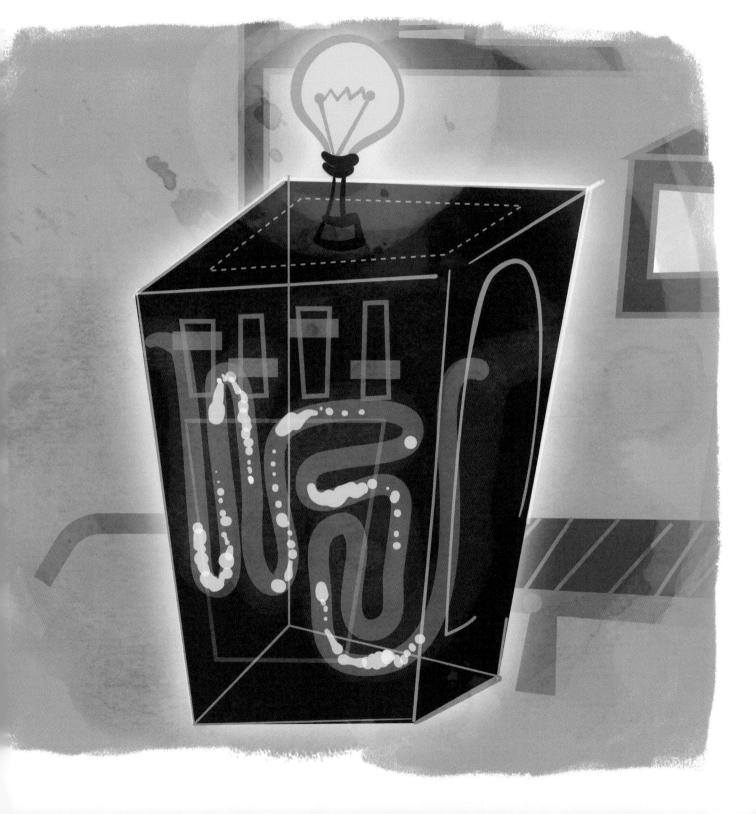

It made the monster dance and jig,
He pulled a lever and twisted a dial.
The top screen, so green and big,
The words made the monster smile.

Up popped the message on the screen,
The monster nodded, wise and sure.
The message was there to be seen,
"You are not in control of the cure."

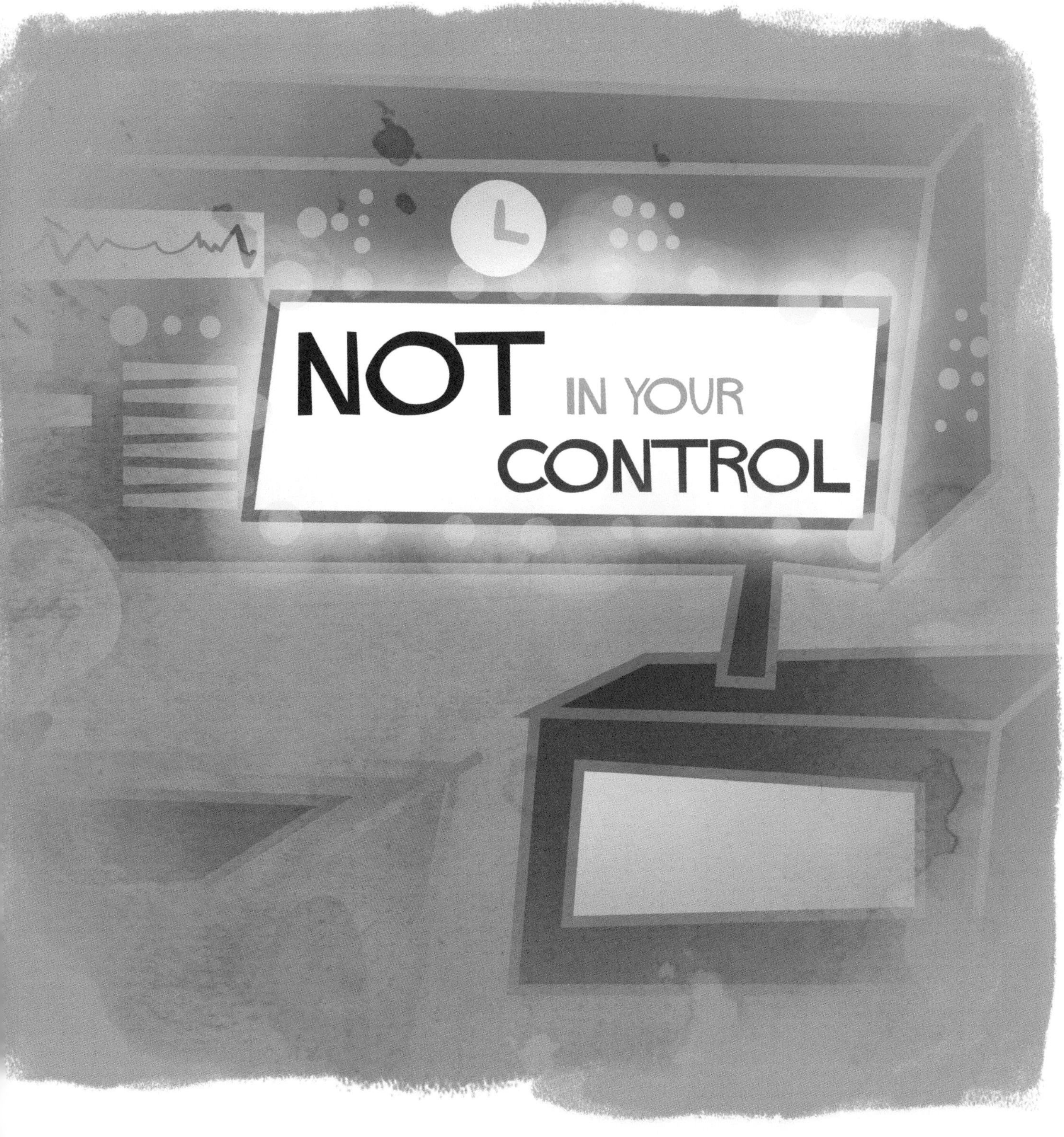
NOT IN YOUR
CONTROL

Tom looked mad and sad once more,
Not in control, what did he mean?
He wanted something to make him sure,
One day, he would be tall and seen.

"Read the screen before you shout!"
The monster urged our little Tom,
Who had started to bubble and pout,
And might blow up, just like a bomb.

"You stood on your pack and became tall,
You really used your head
There is no problem in being small,
You are confident, we listened to what you said.

YOU STOOD ON YOUR PACK AND
BECAME TALL.
YOU REALLY USED YOUR HEAD
THERE IS NO PROBLEM IN BEING SMALL,
YOU ARE CONFIDENT, WE LISTENED TO
WHAT YOU SAID.

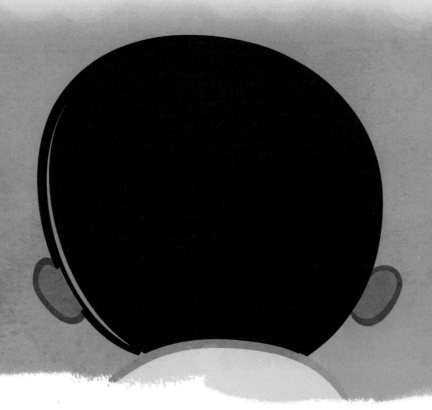

You may not grow taller as you get older,
But you already think and talk.
You really are so much bolder,
Than others as tall as a stalk!"

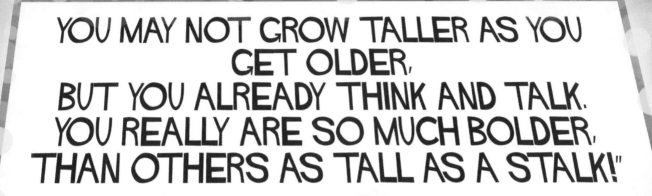

YOU MAY NOT GROW TALLER AS YOU
GET OLDER,
BUT YOU ALREADY THINK AND TALK.
YOU REALLY ARE SO MUCH BOLDER,
THAN OTHERS AS TALL AS A STALK!"

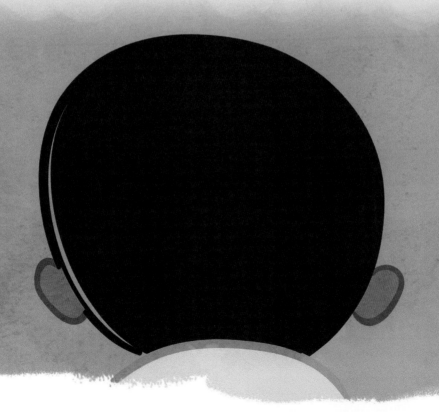

The machine had worked, the monster smiled,
The children too were amazed.
The worries had been slotted and filed,
The answers were rightly praised.

Worries come in many forms
Some are small, we do what we can
Some are big and feel like storms
And then we need a helping hand.

Then, the worries that waste our time
That no one can act to mend
Save your energy, heed our rhyme
Carry on, just talk to a friend.

Printed in Great Britain
by Amazon